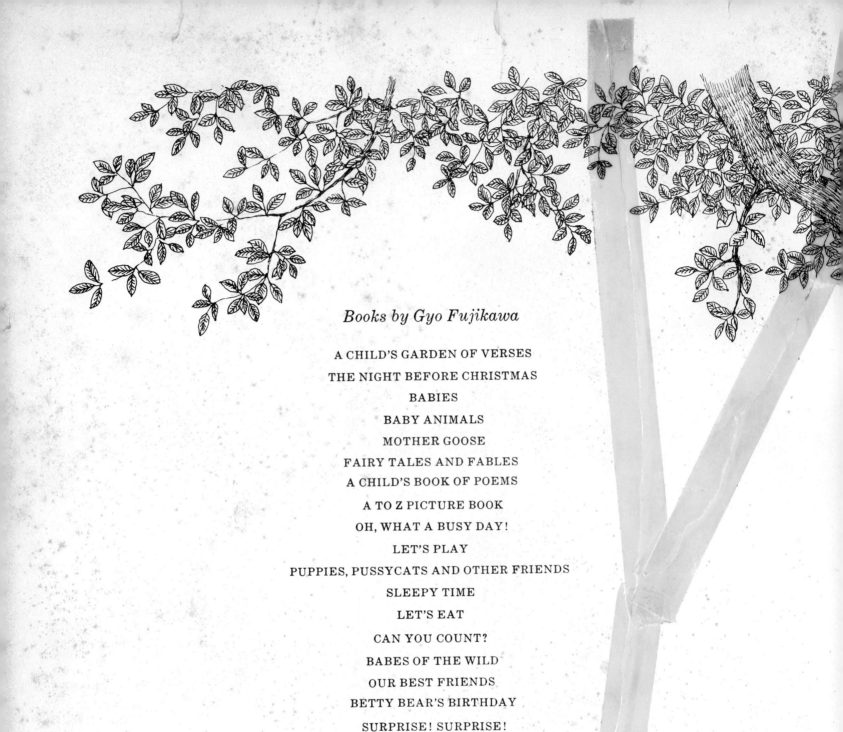

Books by Gyo Fujikawa

A CHILD'S GARDEN OF VERSES

THE NIGHT BEFORE CHRISTMAS

BABIES

BABY ANIMALS

MOTHER GOOSE

FAIRY TALES AND FABLES

A CHILD'S BOOK OF POEMS

A TO Z PICTURE BOOK

OH, WHAT A BUSY DAY!

LET'S PLAY

PUPPIES, PUSSYCATS AND OTHER FRIENDS

SLEEPY TIME

LET'S EAT

CAN YOU COUNT?

BABES OF THE WILD

OUR BEST FRIENDS

BETTY BEAR'S BIRTHDAY

SURPRISE! SURPRISE!

LET'S GROW A GARDEN

MILLIE'S SECRET

MY FAVORITE THING

COME FOLLOW ME . . .

This book belongs to

Mother Goose

Pictures by
Gyo Fujikawa

Grosset & Dunlap · Publishers · New York
Revised Edition

Contents

1982 Printing
Library of Congress Catalog Card Number: 68-29949. ISBN: 0-448-01810-1 (Trade Edition); ISBN: 0-448-03179-5 (Library Edition).

Old Mother Goose

Old Mother Goose,
When she wanted to wander,
Would ride through the air
On a very fine gander.

She lived in a house
That was built in a wood
Where an owl at the door
For a sentinel stood.

She had a son, Jack,
A plain-looking lad;
He was not very good,
Nor yet very bad.

She sent him to market —
A live goose he bought.
"Here, Mother," says he,
"It will not go for naught."

Jack's goose and her gander
Grew very fond;
They'd both eat together,
Or swim in the pond.

Jack found one fine morning,
As I have been told,
His goose had laid him
An egg of pure gold.

Jack ran to his mother,
The news for to tell;
She called him a good boy
And said it was well.

Jack sold his gold egg
To a rascally knave.
Not half of its value
To poor Jack he gave.

And then the gold egg
Was thrown into the sea,
When Jack he jumped in
And got it back presently.

Then Jack went a-courting
A lady so gay,
As fair as the lily,
And sweet as the May.

The knave got the goose,
Which he vowed he would kill,
Resolving at once
His pockets to fill.

The knave and the squire
Came up at his back,
And began to belabor
The sides of poor Jack.

Jack's mother came in
And caught the goose soon,
And mounting its back,
Flew up to the moon.

The Owl

Of all the gay birds that e'er I did see,
The owl is the fairest by far to me,
For all day long she sits in a tree,
And when the night comes, away flies she.

Mary Had a Pretty Bird

Mary had a pretty bird,
    Feathers bright and yellow;
Slender legs, upon my word,
    He was a pretty fellow.

The sweetest notes he always sang,
    Which much delighted Mary;
And near the cage she'd ever sit,
    To hear her own canary.

A Needle and a Thread

Old Mother Twitchett had but one eye,
And a long tail, which she let fly;
And every time she went over a gap,
A bit of her tail she left in a trap.

Ding, Dong, Bell

Ding, dong, bell,
Pussy's in the well.
Who put her in?
Little Johnny Green.
Who pulled her out?
Little Johnny Stout.
What a naughty boy was that
To try to drown poor pussy cat,
Who never did him any harm,
But killed the mice in his father's barn.

Simple Simon

Simple Simon met a pieman
    Going to the fair;
Says Simple Simon to the pieman,
    "Let me taste your ware."

Says the pieman to Simple Simon,
    "Show me first your penny."
Says Simple Simon to the pieman,
    "Indeed, I have not any."

Simple Simon went a-fishing,
    For to catch a whale;
All the water he had got
    Was in his mother's pail.

He went to catch a dickey bird
    And thought he could not fail,
Because he'd got a little salt
    To put upon its tail.

He went to shoot a wild duck,
    But wild duck flew away;
Says Simon, "I can't hit him,
    Because he will not stay."

The Hart

The hart he loves the high wood,
    The hare she loves the hill;
The knight he loves his bright sword,
    The lady loves her will.

To the Snow

Snow, snow faster,
Ally-ally-blaster;
The old woman's plucking her geese,
Selling the feathers a penny a piece.

The Cat and the Fiddle

Hey, diddle, diddle, the cat and the fiddle,
The cow jumped over the moon;
The little dog laughed to see such sport,
And the dish ran away with the spoon.

Tally-Ho!

Tally-Ho! Tally-Ho!
A-hunting we will go!
We'll catch a fox
And put him in a box
And never let him go.

Barber, Barber

Barber, barber, shave a pig,
How many hairs will make a wig?
Four and twenty, that's enough.
Give the barber a pinch of snuff.

Going to Bed

Go to bed late,
Stay very small;
Go to bed early,
Grow very tall.

15

Merry are the Bells

Merry are the bells and merry would they ring,
Merry was myself, and merry could I sing;
With a merry ding-dong, happy, gay, and free,
And a merry sing-song, happy let us be!

Waddle goes your gait, and hollow are your hose,
Noddle goes your pate, and purple is your nose;
Merry is your sing-song, happy, gay, and free,
With a merry ding-dong, happy let us be!

Merry have we met, and merry have we been,
Merry let us part, and merry meet again;
With our merry sing-song, happy, gay, and free,
And a merry ding-dong, happy let us be!

Banbury Fair

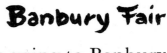

As I was going to Banbury,
    Upon a summer's day,
My dame had butter, eggs and fruit,
    And I had corn and hay.
Joe drove the ox, and Tom the swine,
    Dick took the foal and mare;
I sold them all — then home to dine,
    From famous Banbury fair.

Pussy-Cat Mew

Pussy-Cat Mew jumped over a coal
And in her best petticoat burned a great hole.
Poor pussy's weeping, she'll have no more milk
Until her best petticoat's mended with silk.

Two Comical Folk

In a cottage in Fife
Lived a man and his wife,
Who, believe me, were comical folk;
For, to people's surprise,
They both saw with their eyes,
And their tongues moved whenever they spoke.
When quite fast asleep,
I've been told that to keep
Their eyes open they could not contrive;
They walked on their feet,
And 'twas thought what they eat
Helped, with drinking, to keep them alive.

Penny and Penny

Penny and penny,
Laid up will be many;
Who will not save a penny
Shall never have any.

A Cherry

As I went through the garden gap,
Who should I meet but Dick Redcap!
A stick in his hand, a stone in his throat,
If you'll tell me this riddle, I'll give you a groat.

Pat-a-Cake

Pat-a-cake, pat-a-cake, baker's man,
Bake me a cake as fast as you can.
Pat it and prick it and mark it with T,
And put it in the oven for Tommy and me.

Rock-a-Bye, Baby

Rock-a-bye, baby, on the tree top;
When the wind blows, the cradle will rock;
When the bough breaks, the cradle will fall;
Down will come baby, cradle and all.

March Winds

March winds and April showers
Bring forth May flowers.

19

Queen Anne

Lady Queen Anne she sits in the sun,
As fair as a lily, as white as a swan;
Come taste my lily, come smell my rose,
Which of my maidens do you choose?
The ball is ours and none of yours,
Go to the wood and gather flowers.
Cats and kittens now stay within,
While we young maidens walk out and in.

Solomon Grundy

Solomon Grundy,
Born on a Monday,
Christened on Tuesday,
Married on Wednesday,
Took ill on Thursday,
Worse on Friday,
Died on Saturday,
Buried on Sunday.
This is the end
Of Solomon Grundy.

Nothing

There was an old woman
    And nothing she had,
And so this old woman
    Was said to be mad.
She'd nothing to eat,
    She'd nothing to wear,
She'd nothing to lose,
    She'd nothing to fear,
She'd nothing to ask,
    And nothing to give,
And when she did die,
    She'd nothing to leave.

Rain

Rain, rain, go away,
Come again another day,
Little Johnny wants to play.
Rain, rain, go to Spain,
Never show your face again.

Jack Sprat

Jack Sprat could eat no fat,
His wife could eat no lean;
And so, betwixt them both, you see,
They licked the platter clean.

The Crooked Sixpence

There was a crooked man
    And he went a crooked mile;
He found a crooked sixpence
    Beside a crooked stile;
He bought a crooked cat
    Which caught a crooked mouse,
And they all lived together
    In a little crooked house.

Jeremiah

Jeremiah, blow the fire,
    Puff, puff, puff!
First you blow it gently,
    Then you blow it rough.

Cantaloupes

Cantaloupes! Cantaloupes!
What is the price?
Eight for a dollar,
And all very nice.

The Gossips

Miss One, Two and Three
    Could never agree
While they gossiped around
    A tea-caddy.

The Robins

A robin and a robin's son
Once went to town to buy a bun.
They couldn't decide on plum or plain,
And so they went back home again.

Bobby Shaftoe

Bobby Shaftoe's gone to sea,
Silver buckles on his knee;
He'll come back and marry me,
    Pretty Bobby Shaftoe!

Bobby Shaftoe's fat and fair
Combing down his yellow hair;
He's my love forevermore,
    Pretty Bobby Shaftoe!

Ducks and Drakes

A duck and a drake,
A nice barley cake,
With a penny to pay the old baker;
A hop and a scotch
Is another notch,
Slitherum, slatherum, take her.

BAKER

Jack and Jill

Jack and Jill went up the hill
    To fetch a pail of water.
Jack fell down and broke his crown,
    And Jill came tumbling after.

Then up Jack got and home did trot,
    As fast as he could caper;
Went to bed to mend his head
    With vinegar and brown paper.

Jack and His Fiddle

"Jacky, come and give me thy fiddle,
    If ever thou mean to thrive."
"Nay, I'll not give any fiddle
    To any man alive.
If I should give my fiddle,
    They'll think that I've gone mad;
For many a joyous day
    My fiddle and I have had."

Elsie Marley

Elsie Marley is grown so fine,
She won't get up to feed the swine,
But lies in bed till eight or nine.
    Lazy Elsie Marley.

Ipsey Wipsey

Ipsey Wipsey spider
    Climbing up the spout;
Down came the rain
    And washed the spider out;
Out came the sunshine
    And dried up all the rain;
Ipsey Wipsey spider
    Climbing up again.

Pease Porridge Hot

Pease porridge hot,
    Pease porridge cold,
Pease porridge in the pot,
    Nine days old.
Some like it hot,
    Some like it cold,
Some like it in the pot,
    Nine days old.

To the Bat

Bat, bat, come under my hat,
    And I'll give you a slice of bacon;
    And when I bake, I'll give you a cake,
    If I am not mistaken.

An Old Woman

There was an old woman, and what do you think?
She lived upon nothing but victuals and drink.
Victuals and drink were the chief of her diet,
And yet this old woman could never keep quiet.

Boys and Girls

What are little boys made of, made of?
What are little boys made of?
    Snips and snails,
    And puppy dogs' tails,
That's what little boys are made of.

What are little girls made of, made of?
What are little girls made of?
    Sugar and spice
    And all that's nice,
That's what little girls are made of.

Pussy-Cat, Where Have You Been?

"Pussy-Cat, Pussy-Cat, where have you been?"
"I've been to London to visit the Queen."
"Pussy-Cat, Pussy-Cat, what did you there?"
"I frightened a little mouse under the chair."

Old King Cole

Old King Cole
Was a merry old soul,
And a merry old soul was he;
He called for his pipe
And he called for his bowl,
And he called for his fiddlers three.

Every fiddler
Had a fiddle,
And a very fine fiddle had he;
Oh, there's none so rare
As can compare
With King Cole and his fiddlers three.

Red Sky

Red sky at night,
Shepherd's delight;
Red sky in the morning,
Shepherd's warning.

Baa, Baa, Black Sheep

Baa, baa, black sheep,
    Have you any wool?
Yes, sir, yes, sir,
    Three bags full;
One for the master,
    And one for the dame,
And one for the little boy
    Who lives down the lane.

Sing, Sing

Sing, sing, what shall I sing?
The cat's run away with the pudding string!
Do, do, what shall I do?
The cat has bitten it quite in two.

Hannah Bantry

Hannah Bantry, in the pantry,
Gnawing at a mutton bone;
How she gnawed it,
How she clawed it,
When she found herself alone.

One, Two, Three, Four, Five

One, two, three, four, five,
Once I caught a fish alive,
Six, seven, eight, nine, ten,
Then I let it go again.
Why did you let it go?
Because it bit my finger so.
Which finger did it bite?
The little finger on the right.

Punch and Judy

Punch and Judy
Fought for a pie;
Punch gave Judy
A knock in the eye.
Says Punch to Judy,
"Will you have any more?"
Says Judy to Punch,
"My eye is sore."

Needles and Pins

Needles and pins, needles and pins,
When a man marries, his trouble begins.

The Merchants of London

Hey diddle, dinketty, poppety, pet,
The merchants of London they wear scarlet;
Silk in the collar and gold in the hem,
So merrily march the merchant men.

Play Days

How many days has my baby to play?
Saturday, Sunday, Monday,
Tuesday, Wednesday, Thursday, Friday,
Saturday, Sunday, Monday.
Hop away, skip away,
My baby wants to play;
My baby wants to play every day.

There Was a Rat

There was a rat,
  For want of stairs,
Went down a rope
  To say his prayers.

Little Tom Tucker

Little Tom Tucker
  Sings for his supper.
What shall we give him?
  White bread and butter.
How shall he cut it
  Without any knife?
How shall he marry
  Without any wife?

London Bridge

London Bridge is falling down,
Falling down, falling down;
London Bridge is falling down,
My fair lady.

We must build it up again,
Up again, up again;
We must build it up again,
My fair lady.

Build it up with cotton thread,
Cotton thread, cotton thread;
Build it up with cotton thread,
My fair lady.

Cotton thread will not hold fast,
Not hold fast, not hold fast;
Cotton thread will not hold fast,
My fair lady.

Jacky Jingle

Now what do you think
Of little Jack Jingle?
Before he was married,
He used to live single.

But after he married,
To alter his life,
He left off living single
And lived with his wife.

Will You Lend Me ?

Will you lend me your mare to ride a mile?
No, she is lame leaping over a stile.
Alack! and I must go to the fair,
I'll give you good money for lending your mare.
Oh, oh! say you so?
Money will make the mare to go.

Cock Robin Got Up Early

Cock Robin got up early,
  At the break of day,
And went to Jenny's window
  To sing a roundelay.

He sang Cock Robin's love
  To pretty Jenny Wren,
And when he got unto the end,
  Then he began again.

Three Men in a Tub

Rub-a-dub-dub,
Three men in a tub,
And who do you think they be?
The butcher, the baker,
The candlestick maker,
They all jumped out of a rotten potato,
Turn 'em out, knaves all three!

Bow-Wow

Bow-wow says the dog,
  Mew, mew says the cat,
Grunt, grunt goes the hog,
  And squeak goes the rat.

Whoo-oo says the owl,
  Caw, caw says the crow,
Quack, quack says the duck,
  And what cuckoos say, you know.

So with cuckoos and owls,
  With rats and with dogs,
With ducks and with crows,
  With cats and with hogs,

A fine song I have made,
  To please you, my dear;
And if it's well-sung,
  'Twill be charming to hear.

Queen Caroline

Queen, Queen Caroline,
Washed her hair in turpentine,
Turpentine made it shine,
Queen, Queen Caroline.

This Little Man Lived All Alone

This little man lived all alone,
And he was a man of sorrow;
For, if the weather was fair today,
He was sure it would rain tomorrow.

Shall We Go A-Shearing?

"Old woman, old woman, shall we go a-shearing?"
"Speak a little louder, sir, I'm very hard of hearing."
"Old woman, old woman, shall I kiss you dearly?"
"Thank you very kindly, sir, I hear you very clearly."

Three Ghostesses

Three little ghostesses,
Sitting on postesses,
Eating buttered toastesses,
Greasing their fistesses,
Up to their wristesses,
Oh, what beastesses
To make such feastesses!

Bye, Baby Bunting

Bye, baby bunting,
Daddy's gone a-hunting,
Gone to get a rabbit skin
To wrap the baby bunting in.

The Man in Our Town

There was a man in our town
And he was wondrous wise,
He jumped into a bramble bush
And scratched out both his eyes;
But when he saw his eyes were out,
With all his might and main,
He jumped into another bush
And scratched them in again.

It's Raining

It's raining, it's pouring,
The old man is snoring.
He went to bed with a cold in his head
And he didn't wake up until morning.

Cross-Patch

Cross-patch,
Draw the latch,
Sit by the fire and spin;
Take a cup
And drink it up,
Then call your neighbors in.

Birds of a Feather

Birds of a feather flock together,
And so will pigs and swine;
Rats and mice will have their choice,
And so will I have mine.

Higglety, Pigglety

Higglety, pigglety, pop!
The dog has eaten the mop;
The pig's in a hurry,
The cat's in a flurry,
Higglety, pigglety, pop!

Fears and Tears

Tommy's tears and Mary's fears
Will make them old before their years.

Sing a Song of Sixpence

Sing a song of sixpence,
    A pocket full of rye;
Four-and-twenty blackbirds
    Baked in a pie.

When the pie was opened,
    The birds began to sing;
Wasn't that a dainty dish
    To set before the king?

The king was in his countinghouse,
    Counting out his money;
The queen was in the parlor,
    Eating bread and honey.

The maid was in the garden,
    Hanging out the clothes,
When down came a blackbird
    And snapped off her nose.

Purple Plums

Purple plums that hang so high,
I shall eat you by and by.

Diddlety, Diddlety, Dumpty

Diddlety, diddlety, dumpty,
The cat ran up a plum tree;
Half a crown
To fetch her down,
Diddlety, diddlety, dumpty.

St. Swithin's Day

St. Swithin's Day, if thou dost rain,
For forty days it will remain;
St. Swithin's Day, if thou be fine,
For forty days the sun will shine.

For Want of a Nail

For want of a nail,
    The shoe was lost;
For want of a shoe,
    The horse was lost;
For want of a horse,
    The rider was lost;
For want of a rider,
    The battle was lost;
For want of a battle,
    The kingdom was lost;
And all for the want
    Of a horseshoe nail.

Green Gravel

Green gravel, green gravel,
    Until it grows green,
For the prettiest young fair maid
    That ever was seen;
We'll wash her in new milk
    And clothe her in silk,
And write down her name
    With a gold pen and ink.

Bagpipes

Puss came dancing out of a barn
With a pair of bagpipes under her arm;
She could sing nothing but "Fiddle-de-dee,
The mouse has married the bumblebee."
Pipe, cat; dance, mouse;
We'll have a wedding at our good house.

Pit, Pat

Pit, pat, well-a-day,
Little Robin flew away;
Where can little Robin be?
Gone into the cherry tree.

Three Young Rats

Three young rats with black felt hats,
Three young ducks with new straw flats,
Three young dogs with curling tails,
Three young cats with demi-veils,
Went out to walk with two young pigs
In satin vests and sorrel wigs;
But suddenly it chanced to rain,
And so they all went home again.

The Old Woman in a Shoe

There was an old woman
    Who lived in a shoe.
She had so many children,
    She didn't know what to do.

She gave them some broth,
    Without any bread,
And spanked them all soundly
    And sent them to bed.

The Man Who Had Naught

There was a man and he had naught,
    And robbers came to rob him;
He crept up to the chimney pot,
    And then they thought they had him.

But he got down on t'other side,
    And then they could not find him;
He ran fourteen miles in fifteen days,
    And never looked behind him.

There Was a Little Girl

There was a little girl, and she had a little curl
    Right in the middle of her forehead.
When she was good, she was very, very good,
    And when she was bad, she was horrid.

Diddle, Diddle Dumpling

Diddle, diddle, dumpling, my son John.
Went to bed with his trousers on;
One shoe off and one shoe on,
Diddle, diddle, dumpling, my son John.

Multiplication is Vexation

Multiplication is vexation,
Division is as bad;
The rule of three perplexes me
And practice drives me mad.

Mother Shuttle

Old Mother Shuttle
Lived in a coal-scuttle
Along with her dog and her cat;
What they ate I can't tell,
But 'tis known very well
That not one of the party was fat.

Old Mother Shuttle
Scoured out her coal-scuttle,
And washed both her dog and her cat;
The cat scratched her nose
So they came to hard blows,
And who was the gainer by that?

The Milkmaid

Little maid, pretty maid,
    Whither goest thou?
Down in the forest
    To milk my cow.
Shall I go with thee?
    No, not now.
When I send for thee,
    Then come thou.

Poor Dog Bright

Poor Dog Bright
Ran off with all his might,
Because the cat was after him —
Poor Dog Bright!

Poor Cat Fright
Ran off with all her might,
Because the dog was after her —
Poor Cat Fright!

The Robin

The north wind doth blow
And we shall have snow,
And what will poor robin do then,
    Poor thing?

He'll sit in a barn
And keep himself warm,
And hide his head under his wing,
    Poor thing!

Tom, Tom, the Piper's Son

Tom, Tom, the piper's son,
Stole a pig, and away he run.
The pig was eat, and Tom was beat,
And Tom ran crying down the street.

Harvest

The boughs do shake and the bells do ring,
So merrily comes our harvest in,
Our harvest in, our harvest in,
So merrily comes our harvest in.

We've ploughed, we've sowed,
We've reaped, we've mowed,
We've got our harvest in.

Little Jack Horner

Little Jack Horner
Sat in the corner,
Eating his Christmas pie;
He put in his thumb
And pulled out a plum,
And said, "What a good boy am I!"

Tommy and Bessy

As Tommy Snooks and Bessy Brooks
    Were walking out one Sunday,
Says Tommy Snooks to Bessy Brooks,
    "Tomorrow will be Monday."

Little Blue Ben

Little Blue Ben, who lives in the glen,
Keeps a blue cat and one blue hen,
Which lays of blue eggs a score and ten;
Where shall I find the little Blue Ben?

Elizabeth

Elizabeth, Libby, Betsy and Bess,
They all went together to seek a bird's nest;
They found a bird's nest with five eggs in,
They all took one, and left four in.

The Man in the Wilderness

The man in the wilderness said to me,
"How many strawberries grow in the sea?"
I answered him as I thought good,
"As many as red herrings grow in the wood."

Days in the Month

Thirty days hath September,
April, June and November;
All the rest have thirty-one,
Excepting February alone,
And that has twenty-eight days clear
And twenty-nine in each leap year.

Poll Parrot

Little Poll Parrot
Sat in his garret,
Eating toast and tea;
A little brown mouse
Jumped into the house
And stole it all away.

Two Little Dogs

Two little dogs sat by the fire
Over a fender of coal-dust;
Said one little dog to the other little dog,
"If you don't talk, why, I must."

Saturday Night

On Saturday night I lost my wife,
And where do you think I found her?
Up in the moon, singing a tune,
And all the stars around her.

See-saw, Sacradown

See-saw, sacradown,
Which is the way to London town?
One foot up and the other foot down,
That is the way to London town.

Wibbleton and Wobbleton

From Wibbleton to Wobbleton is fifteen miles,
From Wobbleton to Wibbleton is fifteen miles,
From Wibbleton to Wobbleton,
From Wobbleton to Wibbleton,
From Wibbleton to Wobbleton is fifteen miles.

Candle Saving

To make your candles last for aye,
You wives and maids give ear-o!
To put them out is the only way,
Says Honest John Boldero.

Going to St. Ives

As I was going to St. Ives,
I met a man with seven wives;
Each wife had seven sacks,
Each sack had seven cats,
Each cat had seven kits.
Kits, cats, sacks and wives,
How many were going to St. Ives?

The Moon

I see the moon,
And the moon sees me;
God bless the moon,
And God bless
Me.

The Star

Twinkle, twinkle, little star,
How I wonder what you are!
Up above the world so high,
Like a diamond in the sky.

Girls and Boys, Come Out to Play

Girls and boys,
    Come out to play,
The moon doth shine
    As bright as day.
Leave your supper
    And leave your sleep,
And come with your playfellows
    Into the street.
Come with a whoop,
    Come with a call,
Come with a good will
    Or not at all.
Up the ladder
    And down the wall,
A halfpenny roll
    will serve us all;
You find milk
    And I'll find flour,
And we'll have a pudding
    In half an hour.

Race Starting

Bell horses, bell horses,
What time of day?
One o'clock, two o'clock,
Three and away.

One to make ready,
And two to prepare;
Good luck to the rider,
And away goes the mare.

One for the money,
Two for the show,
Three to make ready,
And four and go.

Hot Cross Buns

Hot cross buns, hot cross buns,
One a penny, two a penny,
Hot cross buns.
If you have no daughters,
Give them to your sons;
One a penny, two a penny,
Hot cross buns.

The Greedy Man

The greedy man is he who sits
And bites bits out of plates,
Or else takes up an almanac
And gobbles all the dates.

That's All

There was an old woman sat spinning,
And that's the first beginning;
She had a calf,
And that's half;
She took it by the tail,
And threw it over the wall,
And that's all.

Pussy Sits Beside the Fire

Pussy sits beside the fire; how can she be so fair?
In walks the little dog; says, "Pussy, are you there?
How do you do, Mistress Pussy, tell me, how do you do?"
"I thank you kindly, little dog; I fare as well as you."

To the Ladybird

Ladybird, ladybird,
 Fly away home,
Your house is on fire
 And your children all gone;
All except one,
 And that's little Ann,
And she has crept under
 The warming pan.

Tommy Trot

Tommy Trot, a man of law,
Sold his bed and lay upon straw;
Sold his straw and slept on grass
To buy his wife a looking-glass.

My Little Dog

Oh where, oh where has my little dog gone?
 Oh where, oh where can he be?
With his ears cut short and his tail cut long,
 Oh, where, oh where is he?

Good Night

Good night,
Sweet repose,
Half the bed
And all the clothes.

Little Maiden

Little maiden, better tarry;
Time enough next year to marry.
Hearts may change,
And so may fancy;
Wait a little longer, Nancy.

Little Bo-Peep

Little Bo-Peep has lost her sheep,
    And can't tell where to find them.
Leave them alone, and they'll come home,
    And bring their tails behind them.

Little Bo-Peep fell fast asleep,
    And dreamed she heard them bleating,
But when she awoke, she found it a joke,
    For they were still a-fleeting.

Then up she took her little crook,
    Determined for to find them;
She found them, indeed, but it made her heart bleed,
    For they'd left all their tails behind them.

It happened one day, as Bo-Peep did stray
    Into a meadow hard by;
There she espied their tails, side by side,
    All hung on a tree to dry.

She heaved a sigh and wiped her eye,
    And over the hillocks she raced;
And tried what she could, as a shepherdess should,
    That each tail be properly placed.

Daffodils

Daffy-down-dilly has come to town
In a yellow petticoat and a green gown.

Niddle-Noddle

Little Robin Redbreast
Sat upon a rail;
Niddle-noddle went his head,
Wiggle-waggle went his tail.

The Queen of Hearts

The Queen of Hearts
She made some tarts,
All on a summer's day;
The Knave of Hearts
He stole some tarts
And took them clean away.

The King of Hearts
Called for the tarts,
And beat the Knave full sore;
The Knave of Hearts
Brought back the tarts,
And vowed he'd steal no more.

Nothing-at-All

There was an old woman called Nothing-at-All,
Who lived in a dwelling exceedingly small;
A man stretched his mouth to its utmost extent,
And down at one gulp house and old woman went.

Davy Dumpling

Davy Davy Dumpling,
    Boil him in the pot;
Sugar him and butter him,
    And eat him while he's hot.

Pins

See a pin and pick it up,
All the day you'll have good luck.
See a pin and let it lay,
Bad luck you'll have all the day.

The Wind

My lady Wind, my lady Wind,
Went round the house to find
  A chink to set her foot in;
She tried the keyhole in the door,
She tried the crevice in the floor,
  And drove the chimney soot in.

To Market, to Market

To market, to market, to buy a fat pig,
  Home again, home again, jiggety jig.
To market, to market, to buy a fat hog,
  Home again, home again, jiggety jog.
To market, to market, to buy a hot bun,
  Home again, home again, market is done.

Taffy was a Welshman

Taffy was a Welshman, Taffy was a thief;
Taffy came to my house and stole a piece of beef;
I went to Taffy's house, Taffy wasn't home;
Taffy came to my house and stole a marrow-bone.

I went to Taffy's house, Taffy wasn't in;
Taffy came to my house and stole a silver pin;
I went to Taffy's house, Taffy was in bed;
I took up the marrow-bone and flung it at his head.

Little Bird

Once I saw a little bird
    Come hop, hop, hop,
And I cried, "Little bird,
    Will you stop, stop, stop?"

I was going to the window
    To say, "How do you do?"
But he shook his little tail
    And away he flew.

Blind Man's Buff

Blind man, blind man,
    Sure you can't see?
Turn round three times,
    And try to catch me.
Turn east, turn west,
    Catch as you can,
Did you think you'd caught me?
    Blind, blind man!

The Milk Maid

"Where are you going, my pretty maid?"
"I'm going a-milking, sir," she said.

"May I go with you, my pretty maid?"
"You're kindly welcome, sir," she said.

"What is your father, my pretty maid?"
"My father's a farmer, sir," she said.

"What is your fortune, my pretty maid?"
"My face is my fortune, sir," she said.

"Then I can't marry you, my pretty maid."
"Nobody asked you, sir," she said.

Hickory, Dickory, Dock

Hickory, dickory, dock!
The mouse ran up the clock;
The clock struck one,
The mouse ran down,
Hickory, dickory, dock!

Lavender's Blue

Lavender's blue, diddle, diddle,
    Lavender's green;
When I am king, diddle, diddle,
    You shall be queen.

Let the birds sing, diddle, diddle,
    And the lambs play;
We shall be safe, diddle, diddle,
    Out of harm's way.

This Little Pig

This little pig went to market;
This little pig stayed at home;
This little pig had roast beef;
This little pig had none;
This little pig cried "Wee, wee, wee,
I can't find my way home."

This Old Man

This old man, he played one,
He played knick-knack on his thumb,
Knick-knack, paddy whack,
Give the dog a bone,
This old man came rolling home.

This old man, he played two,
He played knick-knack on his shoe,
Knick-knack, paddy whack,
Give the dog a bone,
This old man came rolling home.

This old man, he played three,
He played knick-knack on his knee,
Knick-knack, paddy whack,
Give the dog a bone,
This old man came rolling home.

Gregory Griggs

Gregory Griggs, Gregory Griggs,
Had twenty-seven different wigs.
He wore them up, he wore them down,
To please the people of the town;
He wore them east, he wore them west,
But he never could tell which he loved the best.

Fire! Fire!

"Fire! Fire!" said Mrs. Dyer.
"Where? Where?" said Mrs. Dare.
"Down the town," said Mrs. Brown.
"Any damage?" said Mrs. Gamage.
"None at all," said Mrs. Hall.

Banbury Cross

Ride a cock-horse to Banbury Cross,
To see a fine lady upon a white horse;
Rings on her fingers and bells on her toes,
She shall have music wherever she goes.

The Jolly Miller

There was a jolly miller once,
   Lived on the river Dee;
He worked and sang from morn till night,
   No lark so blithe as he.
And this the burden of his song
   Forever used to be,
"I care for nobody — no! not I,
   Since nobody cares for me."

A Nick and a Nock

A nick and a nock
A hen and a cock
And a penny for my master.

Magic Words

Hearts, like doors, will open with ease
To very, very little keys,
And don't forget that two of these
Are "I thank you" and "If you please."

Robin Redbreast

Little Robin Redbreast
    Sat upon a tree,
Up went pussy cat,
    And down went he;
Down came pussy,
    And away Robin ran;
Says little Robin Redbreast,
    "Catch me if you can."

Little Robin Redbreast
    Jumped upon a wall,
Pussy cat jumped after him,
    And almost got a fall;
Little Robin chirped and sang,
    And what did pussy say?
Pussy cat said, "Mew!"
    And Robin jumped away.

Little Miss Muffet

Little Miss Muffet sat on a tuffet,
Eating her curds and whey;
Along came a spider
    who sat down beside her
And frightened Miss Muffet away.

Mary, Mary, Quite Contrary

Mary, Mary, quite contrary,
    How does your garden grow?
With silver bells and cockle shells
    And pretty maids all in a row.

The Muffin Man

Oh, do you know the muffin man?
Oh, do you know his name?
Oh, do you know the muffin man
Who lives in Drury Lane?

Oh, yes, I know the muffin man,
The muffin man, the muffin man,
Oh, yes, I know the muffin man
Who lives in Drury Lane.

Peter White's Nose

Peter White will ne'er go right;
Would you know the reason why?
He follows his nose wherever he goes,
And that stands all awry.

Georgie Porgie

Georgie Porgie, pudding and pie,
Kissed the girls and made them cry;
When the boys came out to play,
Georgie Porgie ran away.

Betty Botter's Batter

Betty Botter bought some butter,
"But," she said, "the butter's bitter;
If I put it in my batter,
It will make my batter bitter,
But a bit of better butter,
That would make my batter better."
So she bought a bit of butter,
Better than her bitter butter,
And she put it in her batter,
And the batter was not bitter.
So t'was better Betty Botter
Bought a bit of better butter.

Hob, Shoe, Hob

Hob, shoe, hob,
Hob, shoe, hob,
Here's a nail and there's a nail,
And that's well shod.

A Week of Birthdays

Monday's child is fair of face,
Tuesday's child is full of grace,
Wednesday's child is full of woe,
Thursday's child has far to go,
Friday's child is loving and giving,
Saturday's child works hard for a living,
And the child that's born on the Sabbath day
Is bonny and blithe, and good and gay.

Goose Feathers

Cackle, cackle, Mother Goose,
Have you any feathers loose?
Truly have I, pretty fellow,
Half enough to fill a pillow.
Here are quills, take one or two,
And down to make a bed for you.

Run, Boys, Run

Rats in the garden, catch 'em, Towser,
Cows in the cornfield, run, boys, run;
Cat's in the cream pot, stop her, now, sir,
Fire on the mountain, run, boys, run.

Hobbledy Hops

Hobbledy Hops,
He made some tops
  Out of the morning glory;
He used the seed —
He did, indeed,
  And that's the end of my story.

As I Was Going Along

As I was going along, long, long,
A-singing a comical song, song, song,
The lane that I went was so long, long, long,
And the song that I sung was as long, long, long,
And so I went singing along.

Old Mother Hubbard

Old Mother Hubbard went to the cupboard
To get her poor dog a bone;
But when she got there, the cupboard was bare,
And so the poor dog had none.

She went to the barber's to buy him a wig;
When she came back, he was dancing a jig.
"Oh, you dear merry Grig! How nicely you're prancing!'
Then she held up the wig, and he began dancing.

She went to the fruiterer's to buy him some fruit;
When she came back, he was playing the flute.
"Oh, you musical dog! You surely can speak!
Come, sing me a song!'' . . . and he set up a squeak.

The dog, he cut capers and turned out his toes;
'Twill soon cure the vapors, such attitude shows.
The dame made a curtsy, the dog made a bow;
The dame said, "Your servant!'' The dog said, "Bow-wow!''

Mary Had a Little Lamb

Mary had a little lamb,
　　Its fleece was white as snow;
And everywhere that Mary went,
　　The lamb was sure to go.

It followed her to school one day,
　　That was against the rule;
It made the children laugh and play
　　To see a lamb at school.

And so the teacher turned it out,
　　But still it lingered near;
And waited patiently about
　　Till Mary did appear.

"Why does the lamb love Mary so?"
　　The eager children cry.
"Why, Mary loves the lamb, you know,"
　　The teacher did reply.

The Pumpkin Eater

Peter, Peter, pumpkin eater,
Had a wife and couldn't keep her;
He put her in a pumpkin shell
And there he kept her very well.

Peter, Peter, pumpkin eater,
Had another, and didn't love her;
Peter learned to read and spell,
And then he loved her very well.

The Spider and the Fly

"Will you walk into my parlor?"
    Said the spider to the fly;
" 'Tis the prettiest little parlor
    That ever you did spy.
The way into my parlor
    Is up a winding stair,
And I have many curious things
    To show when you are there."
"Oh, no, no," said the little fly.
    "To ask me is in vain,
For who goes up your winding stair
    Can ne'er come down again!"

Sneeze On Monday

Sneeze on Monday, sneeze for danger;
Sneeze on Tuesday, kiss a stranger;
Sneeze on Wednesday, get a letter;
Sneeze on Thursday, something better;
Sneeze on Friday, sneeze for sorrow;
Sneeze on Saturday, joy tomorrow.

I Had a Little Husband

I had a little husband,
    No bigger than my thumb;
I put him in a pint-pot
    And there I bade him drum.

I bought a little horse
    That galloped up and down;
I bridled him, and saddled him,
    And sent him out of town.

I gave him some garters
    To garter up his hose,
And a little silk handkerchief
    To wipe his pretty nose.

The Clock

There's a neat little clock,
   In the schoolroom it stands,
And it points to the time
   With its two little hands.

And may we, like the clock,
   Keep a face clean and bright,
With hands every ready
   To do what is right.

If Wishes Were Horses

If wishes were horses,
Beggars would ride;
If turnips were watches,
I'd wear one by my side;
And if IF'S and AND'S
Were pots and pans,
There'd be no work for tinkers!

Jack, Be Nimble

Jack, be nimble; Jack, be quick;
Jack, jump over the candlestick.

The Teeth

Thirty white horses
Upon a red hill;
Now they stamp,
Now they champ,
Now they stand still.

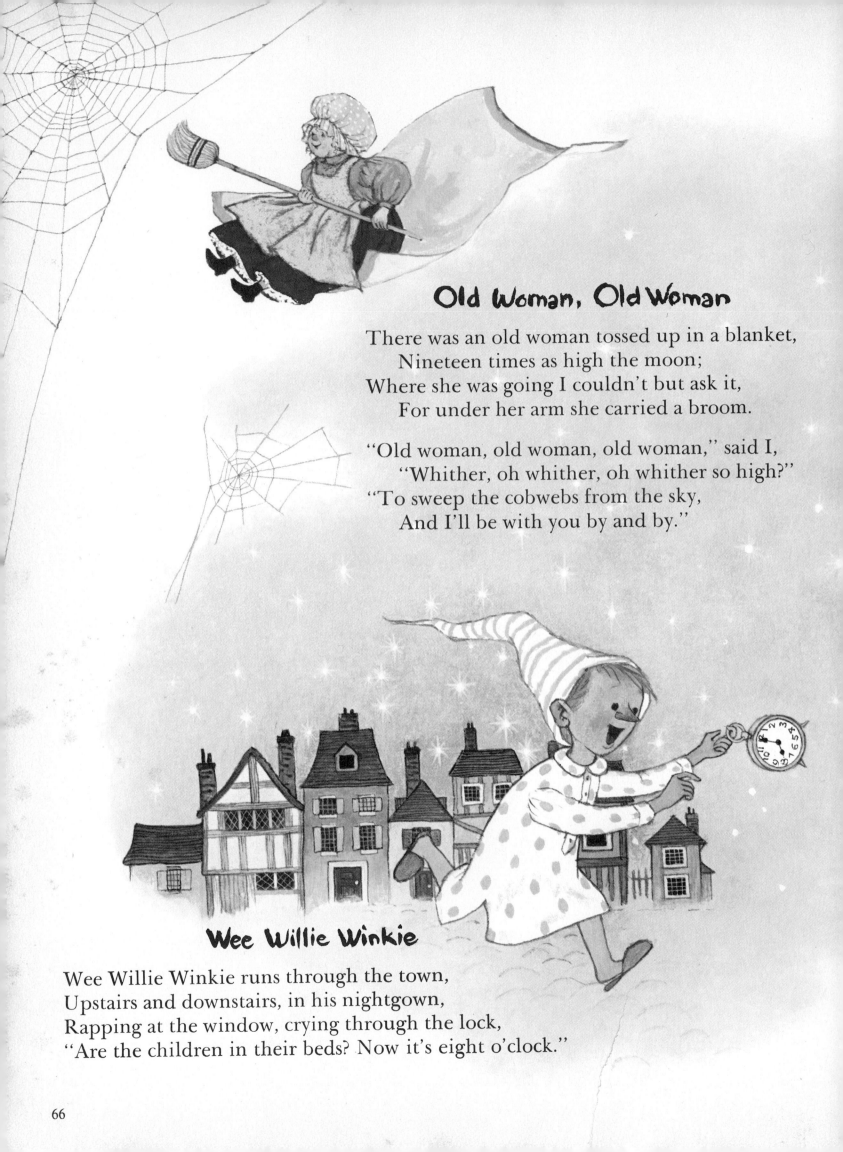

Old Woman, Old Woman

There was an old woman tossed up in a blanket,
    Nineteen times as high the moon;
Where she was going I couldn't but ask it,
    For under her arm she carried a broom.

"Old woman, old woman, old woman," said I,
    "Whither, oh whither, oh whither so high?"
"To sweep the cobwebs from the sky,
    And I'll be with you by and by."

Wee Willie Winkie

Wee Willie Winkie runs through the town,
Upstairs and downstairs, in his nightgown,
Rapping at the window, crying through the lock,
"Are the children in their beds? Now it's eight o'clock."

Star Light

Star light, star bright,
First star I see tonight,
I wish I may, I wish I might,
Have the wish I wish tonight.

Bedtime

The Man in the Moon looked out of the moon,
And this is what he said:
" 'Tis time that, now I'm getting up,
All children are in bed."

A Candle

Little Nanny Etticoat
In a white petticoat
And a red nose;
The longer she stands,
The shorter she grows.

The Mist

A hill full, a hole full,
Yet you cannot catch a bowl full.

Goosey, Goosey, Gander

Goosey, goosey, gander,
    Whither shall I wander?
Upstairs and downstairs
    And in my lady's chamber.

There I met an old man
    Who would not say his prayers;
I took him by the left leg
    And threw him down the stairs.

Hey, My Kitten

Hey, my kitten, my kitten,
    And hey, my kitten, my deary!
Such a sweet pet as this
    Was neither far nor neary.

Here we go up, up, up,
    Here we go down, down, downy;
Here we go backwards and forwards,
    And here we go round, round, roundy.

Polly Flinders

Little Polly Flinders
Sat among the cinders,
Warming her pretty little toes;
Her mother came and caught her,
And spanked her little daughter
For spoiling her nice new clothes.

Leg Over Leg

Leg over leg,
As the dog went to Dover;
When he came to a stile,
Jump, he went over.

Billy Boy

Oh where have you been, Billy Boy, Billy Boy,
Oh where have you been, charming Billy?
I have been to seek a wife,
She's the joy of my life,
She's a young thing and cannot leave her mother.

Can she bake a cherry pie, Billy Boy, Billy Boy,
Can she bake a cherry pie, charming Billy?
She can bake a cherry pie
Quick as the cat can wink its eye,
She's a young thing and cannot leave her mother.

How old is she, Billy Boy, Billy Boy,
How old is she, charming Billy?
Four times six and eight times seven,
Forty-nine plus eleven,
She's a young thing and cannot leave her mother.

My Maid Mary

My maid Mary,
She minds the dairy,
While I go a-hoeing and mowing each morn;
Merrily run the reel,
And the little spinning wheel,
Whilst I am singing and mowing my corn.

Handy Pandy

Handy Pandy, Jack-a-dandy,
Loves plum cake and sugar candy.
He bought some at a grocer's shop,
And out he came, hop, hop, hop.

There Was a Bee

There was a bee
Sat on a wall,
And "Buzz!" said he,
And that was all.

Three Little Kittens

Three little kittens
They lost their mittens,
    And they began to cry,
"Oh, Mother dear,
We sadly fear
    That we have lost our mittens."
"What, lost your mittens!
You naughty kittens!
    Then you shall have no pie."
Mee-ow, mee-ow, mee-ow.
No, you shall have no pie.

The three little kittens
They found their mittens,
    And they began to cry,
"Oh, Mother dear,
See here, see here,
    For we have found our mittens."
"Put on your mittens,
You silly kittens,
    And you shall have some pie."
Purr-r, purr-r, purr-r,
Oh, let us have some pie.

The three little kittens
Put on their mittens
    And soon ate up the pie;
"Oh, Mother dear,
We greatly fear
    That we have soiled our mittens."
"What, soiled your mittens!
You naughty kittens!"
    Then they began to sigh.
    Mee-ow, mee-ow, mee-ow.
    Then they began to sigh.

The three little kittens
They washed their mittens,
    And hung them out to dry;
"Oh, Mother dear,
Do you not hear
    That we have washed our mittens?"
"What, washed your mittens!
Then you're good kittens,
    But I smell a rat close by."
    Mee-ow, mee-ow, mee-ow.
    We smell a rat close by.

Curly-Locks

Curly-Locks, Curly-Locks,
    Wilt thou be mine?
Thou shall not wash dishes
    Nor yet feed the swine;
But sit on a cushion
    And sew a fine seam,
And feed upon strawberries,
    Sugar and cream.

Humpty-Dumpty

Humpty Dumpty sat on a wall,
Humpty Dumpty had a great fall;
All the King's horses and all the King's men
Couldn't put Humpty together again.

Jumping Joan

Here am I,
Little Jumping Joan;
When nobody's with me,
I'm all alone.

Two Little Blackbirds

As I went over the water,
    The water went over me.
I saw two little blackbirds
    Sitting on a tree;
One called me a rascal,
    And one called me a thief,
I took up my little black stick
    And knocked out all their teeth.

Friday Night's Dream

Friday night's dream
On the Saturday told
Is sure to come true,
Be it ever so old.

Tweedledum and Tweedledee

Tweedledum and Tweedledee
   Agreed to have a battle
For Tweedledum said Tweedledee
   Had spoiled his nice new rattle.

Just then flew by a monstrous crow
   As black as a tar barrel,
Which frightened both the heroes so,
   They quite forgot their quarrel.

The Hobby Horse

I had a little hobby horse,
   And it was dapple gray;
Its head was made of pea-straw,
   Its tail was made of hay.

I sold it to a woman
   For a copper groat;
And I'll not sing my song again
   Without another coat.

All Work and No Play

All work and no play makes Jack a dull boy;
All play and no work makes Jack a mere toy.

Three Blind Mice

Three blind mice, see how they run!
They all ran after the farmer's wife,
Who cut off their tails with a carving knife.
Did you ever see such a sight in your life
As three blind mice?

Pop Goes the Weasel

Up and down the City Road,
   In and out the Eagle,
That's the way the money goes,
   Pop goes the weasel!

Half a pound of tuppenny rice,
   Half a pound of treacle,
Mix it up and make it nice,
   Pop goes the weasel!

Every night when I go out,
   The monkey's on the table;
Take a stick and knock it off,
   Pop goes the weasel!

The Kilkenny Cats

There were once two cats of Kilkenny.
Each thought there was one cat too many;
So they fought and they fit,
And they scratched and they bit,
   Till, excepting their nails,
   And the tips of their tails,
Instead of two cats, there weren't any.

Tea Time

Polly put the kettle on,
Polly put the kettle on,
Polly put the kettle on,
   We'll all have tea.

Sukey take it off again,
Sukey take it off again,
Sukey take it off again,
   They've all gone away.

Little Jack Pumpkin Face

Little Jack Pumpkin Face
   Lived on a vine;
Little Jack Pumpkin Face
   Thought it was fine.

First he was small and green,
   Then big and yellow;
Little Jack Pumpkin Face
   Is a fine fellow.

Little Boy Blue

Little Boy Blue,
    Come blow your horn!
The sheep's in the meadow,
    The cow's in the corn.
Where is the boy
    Who looks after the sheep?
He's under a haystack,
    Fast asleep.
Will you wake him?
    No, not I,
For if I do,
    He'll be sure to cry.

Bob Robin

Little Bob Robin,
Where do you live?
Up in yonder wood, sir,
On a hazel twig.

Tommy Tittlemouse

Little Tommy Tittlemouse
Lived in a little house;
He caught fishes
In other men's ditches.

Ride Away, Ride Away

Ride away, ride away,
    Johnny shall ride,
He shall have a pussycat
    Tied to one side;
He shall have a little dog
    Tied to the other,
And Johnny shall ride
    To see his grandmother.

The Cuckoo

The cuckoo comes in April,
He sings his song in May;
    In the middle of June
    He changes his tune,
And then he flies away.

Little Girl

"Little girl, little girl, where have you been?"
"Gathering roses to give to the Queen."
"Little girl, little girl, what gave she you?"
"She gave me a diamond as big as my shoe."

Hay is for Horses

Hay is for horses,
    Straw is for cows,
Milk is for little pigs,
    And wash for old sows.

For Every Evil

For every evil under the sun,
There is a remedy or there is none.
If there be one, try and find it;
If there be none, never mind it.

Do You Love Me?

Do you love me,
Or do you not?
You told me once,
But I forgot.

Christmas is Coming

Christmas is coming,
     The geese are getting fat,
Please to put a penny
     In the old man's hat;
If you haven't got a penny,
     A ha'penny will do,
If you haven't got a ha'penny,
     Then God bless you.

Bedtime

"Come, let's to bed,"
Says Sleepy-head;
"Tarry a while," says Slow;
"Put on the pan,"
Says Greedy Nan,
"Let's sup before we go."

And Now, Good Night

And now, good night;
     Our play is done;
Farewell to each
     And every one.